Let Go of That Toe!

Read other

SPENCER'S
adventures

For Matt Southerland,
a true friend and honest angler.

CONTENTS

Chapter One

Gone to the Dogs

"Wow!" said Spencer. "Our seats are sure high up. This must be the biggest tent in the universe."

"There's nothing like seeing a circus under the big top," said Mr. Burton. "I can still remember my first time."

"That was so long ago, I'll bet they used dinosaurs instead of elephants," joked Spencer.

"And the clowns were cavemen," added Mrs. Burton, laughing.

"Very funny," moaned Mr. Burton.

Suddenly all the lights in the big tent went out. Spencer reached over and gave his sister Amber's hair a good tug. He just couldn't pass up such a good opportunity.

"Ow," snipped Amber. "Spencer Burton, I'll get you for that!"

Spencer's little brother, Jake, let out a squeal of delight as the light from a single spotlight splashed onto the center ring. With a loud drumroll, the ringmaster strutted into the light.

"Ladies and gentlemen," boomed his voice. "Welcome to a night you will not soon forget. You are about to be amazed, thrilled, and terrified by some of the best performers in the universe. Let the show begin!"

Spencer was on the edge of his seat. He was so excited. Every act seemed to be more thrilling than the one before.

When the ringmaster introduced Señor Francisco and his Daring Dogs, Spencer thought it would be the perfect time to take a break.

"I have to use the rest room," whispered Spencer. Mr. Burton and Spencer got up and headed down the stairs. Spencer raced ahead. He wanted to go to the rest room and get back to his seat as fast as he could.

"Slow down," said Mr. Burton. "You're going to fall." But it was too late. As Spencer neared the bottom stair, he tripped. Trying to catch his balance, he crashed into a tough-looking teenager.

The boy gave Spencer a hard shove. The push propelled Spencer forward into a man selling popcorn. Spencer ricocheted off the man and ended up smack in the middle of the center ring, lying on his back.

When Spencer looked up, Señor Francisco and six curious dogs were looking down at him. Spencer swallowed hard and got to his feet. He was just turning to leave when one of Señor Francisco's little poodles ran up his leg to his chest, over his shoulder, and then down his back.

The crowd went wild. They thought Spencer was part of the act. Señor Francisco was always one to take advantage of a good situation. He sat Spencer down in a chair and gave his dogs a signal.

Like doggie missiles, Señor Francisco's dogs took turns flying over Spencer's head. The last dog was a hound dog. He landed in Spencer's lap and gave Spencer a big sloppy lick on the face. The audience laughed and cheered.

The applause was music to Spencer's ears. He took a bow and waved to the crowd. Señor Francisco shook Spencer's hand and escorted him out of the ring.

By the time Spencer got back to his dad, he had forgotten all about going to the bathroom. Mr. Burton gave Spencer a high five and they went back to their seats.

As Spencer watched the rest of the show, he couldn't stop thinking about Señor Francisco's dogs. The few moments he had spent in the spotlight with those animals had changed his life. He was determined to become Señor Spencer and get some daring dogs of his very own.

Chapter Two

It's Show Time

Spencer wasted no time asking for a daring dog of his own. "Dad, may I please have a dog?" he politely asked as they left the circus.

"We already have a dog," replied Mr. Burton.

"Buck's not a dog," whined Spencer.

"Buck's not a dog?" Mr. Burton laughed. "He has a long tail and floppy ears. He scratches and slobbers constantly and has the worst-smelling breath on the planet. Believe me, Spencer, he's a dog."

"What I mean is, he's not a fun dog," replied Spencer. "He's so old. He just lays around the house like a big hairball. I need a dog that has some spunk."

"You mean you want a dog that can do fantastic tricks like the dogs in the circus," said Mr. Burton.

"Yeah," said Spencer excitedly.

"I'm sorry, Spencer, but we are not getting another dog," said Mr. Burton.

Spencer knew better than to argue with his father. When they got home, he went straight to his bedroom. It was time to put Plan B into action. After all, he thought, if at first you don't succeed, try again with the other parent.

Spencer flopped down on his bed and reviewed his options. Whining sometimes worked on his mother. But then, pouting could be a winner, too. Maybe just some good old-fashioned fake crying would do the trick.

"Spencer," called Mrs. Burton. "I need your help in the family room."

A big grin crept across Spencer's face. "It's show time," he said.

Hanging his head low and sticking out his bottom lip, Spencer slowly entered the family room.

"What's the matter, sweetheart?" asked his mother.

"Nothing," mumbled Spencer.

"Oh, honey, something must be the matter," said Mrs. Burton as she put her arm around Spencer.

Spencer bit his lip to keep from smiling. It was perfect. She was taking the bait better than he had even hoped. He let out a big sigh and said, "Dad said that I couldn't get a new dog."

"Spencer, I agree with your father. I

don't think we need another dog," said Mrs. Burton. "Now, would you please get the TV's remote control? It's fallen behind the entertainment center again."

Spencer was always rescuing the remote control. His skinny body was just the right size to squeeze through the bottom opening of the entertainment center.

Spencer got down on his hands and knees and wiggled through the opening. He was about to grab the remote control when he stopped.

"If I had a dog, I'd train him to retrieve the remote for you," said Spencer. "I'd also teach him to wash the windows, set the table, and even do the ironing."

"A window-washing dog would certainly be a sight to see," said Mrs. Burton, chuckling.

Spencer grabbed the remote and wiggled back out of the opening. Handing

the remote to his mother, he said, "My dog would also do the vacuuming, mopping, and shine everybody's shoes once a week."

"What about cooking?" asked Mrs. Burton, giggling. "Will you teach him to cook?"

"Of course," said Spencer.

Mrs. Burton laughed harder and set the remote down on the table next to the lamp. "I tell you what, I'll sit your father down and have a little chat with him. Maybe you could have a pet of your own."

As Mrs. Burton left the room, Spencer threw his fist in the air. He was very excited. When his mom got through with his dad, Spencer was sure that he would be able to have any dog he wanted.

Chapter Three

Señor Spencer

That night, Spencer dreamed about dogs. He dreamed about having a Labrador named Beaker. Spencer trained this dog to be the best retriever in the universe.

At the World Frisbee Championships, Beaker astounded everyone. While people were throwing Frisbees, Spencer marched out with a rocket launcher. He loaded it and let a Frisbee fly. The Frisbee zoomed high in the air and completely out of sight.

Beaker was a blur as he took off after it. He ran up the back of a large man like the man was a ramp. He hit the top of a speeding car and took to the air. His wagging tail propelled him after the Frisbee. When he was just a spot in the clouds, he made the catch.

Beaker, with the Frisbee locked in his jaws, zoomed back to earth. He landed right next to Spencer. The crowd erupted into wild applause. It was the catch of the century. Spencer and his wonder dog were celebrities.

Spencer's dream faded and a new one took its place. This time he owned a St. Bernard named Bernie. Bernie could not only do tricks, he could talk.

Spencer and Bernie even visited the president of the United States at the White House.

Bernie and the president's dog had a long chat. It turned out that the president's dog was actually a lot smarter than the president. He had ideas to solve all the country's problems.

As the night wore on, Spencer had more dreams of fantastic dogs. He dreamed so much about dogs, he started barking in his sleep.

At the breakfast table the next morning, Mr. Burton looked tired. "If that crazy dog next door barks again tonight, I'm calling the police. The barking was so loud it sounded like the dog was right in the house."

"That's funny, I didn't hear a thing," said Spencer, slurping the last of the milk out of his cereal bowl.

As Spencer was leaving for school, his mother stopped him at the door. "You'll want to hurry home from school today," she said, smiling. "Your father and

I have a little surprise for you."

That little surprise could mean only one thing. Spencer was going to get a dog of his own. He felt like dancing all the way to school.

Spencer wanted the day to zoom by, but it seemed like everything was stuck in slow motion. The morning took forever. The afternoon seemed like it would never end.

It was no use trying to concentrate on schoolwork. Every one of Spencer's thoughts was dedicated to his new dog.

He was doodling pictures of dogs on his notebook when Miss Bingham spoke up. "Spencer, are you with us? It seems you're having a hard time focusing today."

"I'm sorry," said Spencer. "It's just that I'm real excited about my new dog."

"Would you like to tell the class about your pet?" asked Miss Bingham.

"Well, he's the smartest, happiest, fastest, best-looking dog in the galaxy," said Spencer. "He can do tricks that would amaze you."

Rex raised his hand. "Miss Bingham, is it all right if Spencer brings this un-believably awesome dog to class for us all to see?"

"I have an even better idea," replied Miss Bingham. "Tomorrow is the school's talent show. It sounds like Spencer and this miracle dog just might be the show-stopper. What about it, Spencer? Could you and your dog do some tricks?"

Without even thinking, Spencer said, "You bet! My act will be Señor Spencer and His Wonder Dog."

The class started chanting, "*Woof. Woof. Woof.*"

"All right, class, that's enough," said Miss Bingham. "Spencer, we're expecting great things out of you and your dazzling dog."

"No sweat," said Spencer, grinning.

The ringing of the bell was the start signal for Spencer's race home. He couldn't wait to see the dog of his dreams.

Chapter Four

Shell-Shocked

Spencer was out of breath as he raced into the yard. This was going to be one of the happiest moments of his life. He hoped to hear barking as he threw open the front door, but the house was quiet.

"Mom! Dad!" shouted Spencer. There was no answer. "They must not have gotten home yet," said Spencer, trying to catch his breath.

When he got to his bedroom, Spencer

stopped dead in his tracks. There was a note taped to the closed door. *Warning! Beware of new pets. Enter this room at your own risk.*

"This is better than Christmas," said Spencer. He opened the door a crack and peeked in. Spencer's parents were sitting on his bed. They were leaning over, looking at something in a cardboard box.

Pushing the door open, Spencer popped into the room. He was practically bouncing as he headed for his bed.

When she spotted Spencer, Mrs. Burton threw her arms in the air and announced, "SURPRISE!"

As he looked into the box, Spencer's eyes grew as big as saucers.

What he saw wasn't fluffy or furry. It didn't have floppy ears or a wagging tail. It wasn't panting or slobbering. It wasn't even a dog. It was a TURTLE!

Spencer was *shell-shocked*. He couldn't believe it. He had wished for a wonder dog and what he got was a miniature army helmet with legs.

"He's yours," blurted out Mrs. Burton excitedly. "We were going to get you a dog, but when we got to the pet store, this little guy just seemed to have your name written all over him."

Spencer looked at the shell. It was the size of a soup bowl and it definitely didn't have his name on it.

"Let's leave these two buddies alone," said Mr. Burton. As the door shut behind his parents, Spencer picked up the turtle. He was about to tell his new pet exactly what he thought of him when his sister Amber called, "SPENCER, the phone is for you."

"Who is it?" groaned Spencer. He didn't feel like talking to anyone.

"It's your friend Josh," said Amber.

"I'll get it in the living room," yelled Spencer, heading down the hall. He set his turtle on the couch and picked up the phone.

"Señor Spencer, what did you name your wonder dog?" asked Josh without even saying hello.

Spencer couldn't bring himself to tell Josh the sad news. "I haven't named him yet," he said.

"If he's fast, you could name him Lightning," suggested Josh.

"Well, he's not all *that* fast," said Spencer, as he looked at the turtle slowly creeping across the couch.

"Can I come over and see him do a few tricks?" asked Josh.

"Now isn't a good time," grumbled Spencer. "He's feeling a little sluggish."

"The whole class is counting on your new dog to be the star of the talent show," said Josh.

"Don't worry," replied Spencer. "I'll see you tomorrow." Spencer hung up the phone, grabbed his pet, and headed back to his room. Amber met him in the hall. When Spencer saw the way she was smiling, he knew there was going to be trouble.

"Get out of my way," ordered Spencer.

"Is your new dog feeling a little sluggish today?" asked Amber.

"You dirty rat," said Spencer. "You listened to my private phone conversation." He set his turtle down on the carpet and prepared for battle.

Amber turned to run, but Spencer grabbed her shirt. He had one arm wrapped around Amber's neck when she screamed, "My toe! My toe! It's trying to rip off my toe!"

"What?" said Spencer, loosening his grip. Looking down, he saw his turtle had one of Amber's toes in its mouth.

Amber shook her foot wildly, but the turtle would not turn her loose.

"He's trying to eat me!" bellowed Amber.

"He can't eat you," shouted Spencer. "He doesn't have any teeth!" Spencer reached down and pried his turtle off his sister's toe.

Amber's toe was perfectly fine, but that didn't stop her from grabbing her foot and hopping down the hall. "Spencer and his turtle are trying to kill me!" she yelled as she bounced into the kitchen.

Spencer quickly grabbed his pet and headed out the front door. He'd only had his turtle for ten minutes and already he was in turtle trouble.

Chapter Five

Turtle Ball

Spencer and his turtle headed for Shriner's Park. It was two blocks away and Spencer thought it would be a good place to hide out.

Racing into the park, Spencer plopped down behind some bushes. "Any critter that would help me attack my crummy sister can't be all bad," said Spencer. "You are a mean, green, biting machine. I'm naming you Jaws."

Spencer laid down in the grass. He put his hands behind his head and closed his eyes. While Spencer daydreamed, Jaws headed out. Amber's toe had left a bad taste in his mouth and he needed something to wash it out.

Jaws was making good time, for a turtle, when he was discovered by a group of seventh-grade boys. Even a turtle knows that a seventh-grade boy is one of the most dangerous creatures in the universe. Jaws stopped moving and sucked his head deep into his shell.

"Hey, look!" shouted a redheaded boy. "I found a big green potato."

"That's no spud, you doofus," called out a boy wearing a Dallas Cowboys football jersey. "That's a turtle."

"Cool," said the redhead, picking up Jaws. He tapped on the top of the shell. "Hello, anybody home?"

"Give him to me," said the football player, grabbing the turtle.

"Anybody up for some turtle ball?" the boy said, laughing. Soon six boys were in a football formation. That's when Spencer came along.

"Any of you guys seen a turtle?" asked Spencer.

"Nope," called out the redhead. "But we found a nifty new ball." Spencer stared in disbelief. A boy was about to hike Jaws to the quarterback.

"Hey, that's not a ball. That's my turtle!" shouted Spencer.

The quarterback called out, "Forty-three green. Hut. Hut. Hut." He took Jaws from the center and faded back.

The receiver started to race down the field. Like a rocket, Spencer took off after him. The quarterback let Jaws fly. He was sailing through the air in a perfect spiral.

Spencer found speed that he didn't know he had. His feet felt like they were turbocharged. Jumping onto a park bench, Spencer launched himself into the air. He sailed right past the receiver's reach and snatched the turtle in midair.

Coming down in a flower bed, Spencer kept pouring it on. The seventh-graders were hot on his trail.

"Get that little creep!" shouted the red-head.

Spencer left the park and headed down Basil Street. When he turned onto Almo Avenue, he spotted an old wooden fence. Like a scared squirrel, Spencer scrambled over the rickety fence before the seventh-graders came around the corner.

On the other side, Spencer listened as the posse of big boys raced by. He let out a sigh of relief and sat down.

Spencer took off his left shoe and

sock. During the escape he had gotten a rock in his shoe. He pounded on the shoe, but nothing came out. He started to shake the sock when he felt a tug on his second toe. Jaws had Spencer's toe in his mouth and was not letting go.

"Hey!" said Spencer loudly. "Let go of that toe!" He reached down and took hold of the turtle. Jaws started to pull his head into the shell.

"You can't take my toe in there," snapped Spencer. Jaws put up a good fight. Spencer rolled around wrestling with his stubborn pet.

The tug-of-war over Spencer's toe suddenly stopped when the fighters heard an evil growling sound. Looking up, Spencer saw the meanest-looking Doberman pinscher that ever walked the planet.

The dog's teeth looked like daggers as he curled up his top lip. Spencer was shaking so hard, he couldn't stand up.

He was about to become a human doggie biscuit. Jaws let go of Spencer's toe and prepared for battle.

The Doberman made his move like a shark. He lunged with his bright teeth shining in the sunlight. He was going to tear Spencer to shreds.

As the mighty dog snapped his mouth shut, he suddenly began yelping. He had ended up with a mouthful of turtle. Jaws' hard shell broke off three of the deadly dog's teeth. Whimpering like a scared puppy, the Doberman ran back to the doghouse with his tail between his legs.

"Way to go, Jaws!" shouted Spencer. "You showed that mutt who was boss!"

Spencer picked up the broken teeth and put them in his pocket. He started yelling at the dog's house. "What's the matter? Scared of a little turtle?"

The big dog came out of the house

again. He was followed by two of his closest friends. They were ready for dinner and Spencer was the main course.

When Spencer looked down, he saw Jaws squeezing under the fence. The mean, green, biting machine was getting out of there.

"Wait for me!" shouted Spencer. He grabbed his shoe and scrambled over the fence just as the dogs charged.

Chapter Six

You've Got to Be Joking

Spencer was still breathing hard from climbing over the fence as he put on his sock and shoe. Picking up Jaws, he headed straight for Josh Porter's house. He couldn't wait to introduce Jaws to his best friend.

Josh was in his front yard when he spotted Spencer. "Howdy, partner," he called out. "What you got there?"

"Something awesome," answered Spencer.

"It looks like a turtle!" exclaimed Josh. "You'd better give him to me. I've heard that turtles and dogs don't get along. You wouldn't want your new dog to — "

"Josh, this *is* my new dog," interrupted Spencer.

"That lizard with a hard hat is not a dog," said Josh.

"I know Jaws isn't a dog," said Spencer. "I thought I was going to get a dog, but then my parents bought me this turtle instead."

"There's only one problem," said Josh. "Miss Bingham signed you and your wonder dog up for the talent show."

"I know," moaned Spencer. "I need you to help me think of an awesome trick for Jaws to do."

"Turtle tricks aren't exactly my specialty, but I'm sure two great minds like ours can come up with something," said Josh.

The minutes ticked by and the combined brainpower of the boys came up with nothing.

Finally Josh said, "I can't think of one thing that a turtle could do in a show. I don't think turtles are very talented."

"Don't say that!" said Spencer.

The front door of Josh's house opened and out came Josh's sister, Ellen.

Josh whispered to Spencer, "My sister is kind of grouchy today. She says she's having a bad hair day."

"What does that mean?" asked Spencer.

"Have a look for yourself," answered Josh.

Spencer stood up and looked at Ellen, who was standing on the porch. Her hair looked like she had stuck her finger in a light socket. It was frizzy and wild.

"Mom, do you have any mousse for my hair?" asked Ellen.

"It's in the top drawer in my bathroom," answered Mrs. Porter from her garden.

When Ellen went back inside, Spencer asked Josh, "How does your sister get her hair to look so goofy?"

"It's easy for her," replied Josh. "She does it all the time."

"Maybe she could fix my hair like that for the talent show," said Spencer. "Then Jaws and I could be a comedy team. Do you know any good turtle jokes?"

"You could balance Jaws on your head and say that you couldn't find any mousse so you used a turtle instead," Josh said with a laugh.

"I like it," replied Spencer, picking up his turtle. He set Jaws on top of his head, but the turtle kept sliding off.

"This won't work." Spencer sighed.

"Just a minute," said Josh. He ran into the house and came back with a big roll of tape. Josh taped Jaws to the top of Spencer's head.

"Wonderful!" exclaimed Spencer. He moved around the yard with ease and the turtle stayed right in place. "Josh Porter, you are a genius. All I need now are some more dynamite turtle jokes."

"No problem," said Josh. "Knock-knock."

"Who's there?" said Spencer.

"Shell," said Josh.

"Shell who?" Spencer asked.

"Shell I come in now?" replied Josh.

Both boys started laughing. "Do you have any more?" asked Spencer.

"Sure," replied Josh. "What do you get if you cross a turtle with a clock?"

"I don't know," replied Spencer.

"You get a hard time," said Josh.

"I get it," said Spencer, laughing. "Your

jokes are great. When Jaws and I become famous and join the circus, you can be our manager."

"You got it," said Josh. "But first you two'd better go and practice for the talent show tomorrow."

"Don't worry about us," said Spencer confidently. "With a turtle taped to my head, I feel I can do anything."

Chapter Seven

Shelling Out the Big Bucks

When Spencer got home, he cut through the flower bed to the window of his room.

Spencer reached up and took the turtle off the top of his head. He patted his pet's shell and said, "Jaws, if you're going to hang out with me you should know it isn't always safe to go through the front door."

Spencer lifted the window and climbed into his room.

Sitting on the bed waiting for him were both of his parents and Amber. Amber's foot was bandaged and resting on a pillow. Spencer turned around quickly and headed for the window.

"Where do you think you're going?" asked Mr. Burton.

"I just remembered I left something at the park," replied Spencer.

"Spencer, Amber informs us that the seemingly harmless pet we bought you is actually a killer attack turtle. Is that true?" asked Mrs. Burton.

"Absolutely not!" insisted Spencer. "Amber had spilled some jelly on her toe and Jaws was just trying to lick it off. She should wash her feet more often."

Amber screamed, "I'll have you know that I have the cleanest toes on this block! That turtle of yours is dangerous. He should be locked up."

"Calm down, Amber," said Mr. Burton firmly. "Spencer, we've decided that the turtle was not such a good idea. We're going to take it back to the pet store."

"What?" gasped Spencer. "You can't take Jaws back. He saved my life today."

"Spencer, your sister may have been angry, but she would never try to kill you," said his mother sternly.

"Not her," said Spencer, "a Doberman pinscher attacked me. Jaws used his razor-sharp reflexes to save me. The killer dog broke three of his teeth on Jaws' shell."

"HELLO," called out Amber. "Have you lost your mind? Turtles do not have razor-sharp reflexes. I don't believe one word of your lame story. That blood-thirsty dog was probably a very old poodle that thought you were a fire hydrant."

"Oh, yeah, then what are these?" asked Spencer. He pulled the broken teeth out of his pocket and showed them to everyone.

"Oh, my," gasped Mrs. Burton. She took one of the teeth from Spencer. "This thing is sharp. I'm certainly glad it bit your turtle instead of you."

Mr. Burton picked up Jaws and patted his shell. "You are one terrific turtle."

"Wait a minute!" yelled Amber. "I'm the one who got hurt today. Those two almost killed me and you're treating them like heroes. Look at my toe. It hurts."

"Oh, Amber, your toe is fine," said Mrs. Burton, giving Spencer a hug.

Spencer wiggled out of his mother's tight grip and announced, "Tomorrow is the school talent show and Jaws and I are going to be the stars."

Mrs. Burton's face burst into a smile. "You can count on me and your father to be in the audience. We wouldn't miss this for anything."

Mr. Burton and Mrs. Burton left Spencer's room arm in arm. Amber followed her parents. She was still sputtering like a boiling teakettle.

That night, Spencer dreamed about the big show. The minute Spencer and Jaws walked onstage the crowd went wild. Spencer's hair was sticking straight up and Jaws was incredible. He was poking his head out and making faces at the crowd.

The jokes flew fast and furious. With each zinger the crowd laughed harder. By the time the act was over, people were holding their sides and a few were rolling on the floor.

As the dynamic duo left the stage, they were mobbed by reporters.

"You two were fantastic," commented a beautiful lady reporter. "Do you have any movie deals coming up?"

Spencer started to answer when a big man with a black hat marched up to the front of the room. "Yes, they do," he said loudly. "That is, if they are interested in becoming fabulously famous and wildly wealthy. I'm making a movie called *The Tortoise and the Hair.* I want these two to be the stars."

"Where do we sign?" blurted out Spencer. Jaws' little green head was bobbing up and down with excitement.

Spencer woke up in the morning with stars in his eyes. He knew that today was going to be fantastic.

Chapter Eight

The Big Day

"What's for breakfast?" asked Spencer as he bounded into the kitchen.

"Pancakes with blueberry syrup," answered Mrs. Burton. She brought a platter of golden pancakes over and set them right in front of Spencer.

Spencer wolfed down three pancakes and gulped down two glasses of milk. He wiped his mouth and asked, "Dad, do we have any Turtle Wax? I want Jaws' shell looking its best for the big show."

Mr. Burton gave Spencer a big smile. "I don't think wax would be very healthy for your turtle's shell. Why don't you just buff it with a soft towel?"

Soon Spencer had his turtle's shell shining like a bowling ball. He put Jaws in a shoe box and headed out the door.

Miss Bingham was at her desk when Spencer entered the classroom. "Spencer, I'm glad to see you," she said, smiling. "In the faculty meeting this morning, Mr. Warner was very worried. It seems that some of the acts he was counting on for the talent show fell through.

"I told him not to worry because Señor Spencer and his Wonder Dog would save the day. Are your parents bringing your dog over later?"

"No," said Spencer. "He's in this box."

Miss Bingham stared at Spencer's backpack. "Well, he is certainly very tiny and very quiet."

Spencer laughed. "Actually, my wonder dog turned out to be a terrific turtle." He pulled Jaws out and set him on Miss Bingham's desk.

"We've worked up a comedy routine," said Spencer.

Miss Bingham looked worried. "I hope it's good. I've been telling everyone what a wonderful act you have."

"Don't worry," said Spencer. "My turtle and I will bring the house down."

When Josh showed up, Spencer quickly asked, "When is your sister showing up to fix my hair?"

"She's not," said Josh. "She has cheerleading practice today. I'm sure the jokes will pull you through."

"They'd better." Spencer sighed. "I'm

not taking any chances of forgetting them. I wrote the jokes down on the palms of my hands."

"Good thinking, Señor Spencer," replied Josh.

The talent show was going to be during the last hour of school. Spencer couldn't wait for the big moment to arrive. He remembered how good the applause at the circus had sounded. He couldn't wait to hear that kind of cheering again.

About twenty minutes before show time, Mr. Warner came into Miss Bingham's classroom. He was barefoot and wearing white karate clothes. Everyone gasped when he entered the room.

"Wow," blurted out T.J. "Mr. Warner, I didn't know you were a ninja."

Mr. Warner laughed. "I'm not a ninja; I have a brown belt in karate."

Rex raised his hand and said, "I

thought there were only black belts in karate."

"Actually, there are many different colors of belts you can earn. It all depends on which skills you have mastered," explained Mr. Warner. "For my act in the talent show, I'm going to break some boards using only my hands, feet, and head."

"That's going to be awesome," said Rex.

"I hope so," said Mr. Warner. "Spencer, I came to get you. It's time to get ready for the talent show. Miss Bingham has informed me that you didn't bring your wonder dog but instead you have a very funny turtle."

"His name is Jaws," replied Spencer. "And we have worked up a very funny comedy routine."

"Great," said Mr. Warner. "This show could use a few laughs."

Spencer picked up Jaws and followed the principal. As they walked down the hall, Jaws couldn't take his eyes off Mr. Warner's toes. They looked like a tootsie buffet and Jaws was in the mood for lunch.

Chapter Nine

Mr. Warner the Ninja

Mr. Warner led Spencer to the back of the stage where the other contestants were waiting. Everyone looked very nervous. Everyone, that is, except Jaws.

Spencer got tired of standing and looked around for somewhere to sit. He spotted a very clean board resting between two blocks.

This must be one of the boards Mr. Warner is going to bust, thought Spencer as he sat down on the wood. His rear end had barely touched it when the board broke in half.

"Wow, that isn't a very strong board," mumbled Spencer. When he picked up the pieces, he noticed that they were very light.

"I'll bet Mr. Warner didn't know he had been given such flimsy wood," said Spencer to his turtle. "I'm sure a brown belt like Mr. Warner wants to only bust really strong boards."

Spencer gathered up all of Mr. Warner's flimsy wood and headed for the custodian's room. Luckily, Mr. Bench was in his room working on some bookcases.

"Mr. Bench," said Spencer, "Mr. Warner needs some really strong wood for the talent show. Do you have any?"

"You're in luck," said Mr. Bench, grinning. "I just built this bookcase and I have some scrap pieces of really sturdy oak left over. In fact, they are about the same size as that balsa wood you have there."

"Great!" said Spencer. "Can I have some?"

"Sure," said the custodian.

Spencer filled his arms with the wood and went back to the stage. He neatly stacked the boards and then peeked around the curtains. The auditorium was beginning to fill up. Spencer smiled when he saw his parents sitting in the back of the room.

Spencer spotted Josh sitting on the end of the tenth row. Spencer was about to stick his head out and make a few funny faces when he felt someone touch his shoulder. It was Mr. Warner.

"Spencer, come and join us," said the principal. "I want to say a few things to all the performers before the show begins."

Everyone gathered around Mr. Warner. "Students, in show business before a show, the performers say to each other 'Break a leg.' That means give it your best. I want each of you to try to relax and break a leg."

Mr. Warner's words of encouragement didn't seem to help the performers. Each act seemed more boring than the one before it. The talent show dragged on and the audience grew restless. Finally there were only two acts left: Mr. Warner and Spencer.

Spencer was taping his turtle to the top of his head when the master of ceremonies announced Mr. Warner. Spencer quickly turned around to see Mr. Warner's act. He couldn't wait to see the expression on Mr. Warner's face when he discovered that he had good boards instead of those flimsy ones.

Mr. Warner slowly moved around the

stage. He was making karate noises while chopping and kicking in the air. He circled the stage and then stopped behind the board that was resting between the blocks. With a loud yell, Mr. Warner hit the board. The yell he made after hitting the wood was much louder than the one he made before hitting it. The board didn't break. It didn't crack. It didn't even move.

Mr. Warner's eyes grew big. He looked at the board and then at his hurt hand. The audience was silent.

Like a true ninja, Mr. Warner didn't give up. He raised his right foot high in the air. He yelled and his foot came crashing down on the board. This time there was a loud cracking sound. But it must have been Mr. Warner's foot, because the board appeared to be unhurt.

The principal bit his lip and limped around in a small circle. He was not going to let this board get the best of him. One more time, he got behind the stubborn piece of wood.

Mr. Warner slowly lowered his head to the wood. Some members of the audience held their breath, while others let out a gasp. The principal raised his head and then quickly crashed it down on the wood. The board didn't budge.

When Mr. Warner stood up, his eyes were crossed. He shook his head a couple of times and slowly walked offstage. He went right past Spencer and sat down in a chair.

Suddenly Spencer heard the words he had been waiting for: "Give a big Crestview Elementary School welcome to Señor Spencer and Jaws the Wonder Turtle."

Chapter Ten

The Toe That Saved the Show

Spencer hurried onto the stage. The microphone made a loud squeaking sound as he started to speak. "You are probably wondering why I have a turtle on my head," said Spencer. "We were out of mousse, so I used a turtle instead."

The room was silent. Not one person laughed. Spencer became so nervous, his hands began to sweat. When he looked down to read his next joke, all that was left was a black ink spot.

Spencer's mind whirled. He tried to remember one of the jokes, but he couldn't. His mind was a complete blank.

Spencer couldn't speak or move. He searched the audience for anyone who might be able to help. Miss Bingham was looking down, shaking her head. His mom was biting her lip and his dad was staring at the ceiling.

Amber was hiding her face in her hands. She was sure the family would have to move to another town when this disaster was finally over.

Spencer reached up and took hold of Jaws. He pulled the turtle loose and looked at his green pet. He thought that looking at Jaws might jog his memory.

Jaws' head was pulled back deep into his shell. He was no help at all. Spencer set the turtle down on the floor.

Suddenly Mr. Warner appeared next to Spencer. He was still feeling woozy, but he had to get Spencer off the stage. He didn't want the audience to have to witness another disaster.

As Mr. Warner leaned over to whisper to Spencer, Jaws stuck his head out of his shell. His little green eyes grew big when he saw what was right in front of him.

Like a row of juicy hot dogs, Mr. Warner's toes were lined up just waiting to be bitten. Jaws wasted no time. He chose Mr. Warner's little toe and chomped down.

Mr. Warner's entire body went stiff. He gave his foot a little flip, but Jaws held fast. Then Mr. Warner shook his foot a little harder. It was like a carnival ride for Jaws.

Spencer leaned over and loudly said, "Let go of that toe!"

People in the audience started to snicker. That made Mr. Warner nervous and he started shaking his foot harder. The faster he moved his foot, the tighter Jaws held on. Soon the entire audience was roaring with laughter.

Mr. Warner was bouncing around the stage on one leg and shaking the other foot in the air. Jaws was holding on for dear life and Spencer was chasing after them, yelling, "Let go of that toe!"

Finally Mr. Warner raised his foot high in the air. It was directly over the board he had tried to break earlier. With all his strength, Mr. Warner crashed his foot down on the board. The jolt sent Jaws soaring in the air.

Spencer took off after his flying pet. He caught Jaws just before the turtle hit the floor. When Spencer looked back at Mr. Warner, the principal was grinning from ear to ear. His big kick had busted the hard wood right in half. He held the broken board up for the audience to see.

The crowd erupted in applause. They gave Spencer, Jaws, and Mr. Warner a standing ovation.

While they were taking their bows, Spencer said to Mr. Warner, "I think we're a hit."

"You're right," replied Mr. Warner. "And we owe it all to your turtle and my toe."

Spencer and Mr. Warner started to laugh and took one last bow as the crowd went wild.

About the Author

Gary Hogg has always loved stories and has been creating them since he was a boy growing up in Idaho.

Gary is also a very popular storyteller. Each year he brings his humorous tales to life for thousands of people around the United States.

He lives in Huntsville, Utah, with his wife, Sherry, and their children, Jackson, Jonah, Annie, and Boone.